★ Knight of the Cape ★

Don't miss the other books in the Definitely Dominguita series!

#2: *Captain Dom's Treasure*

Coming soon:
#3: *All for One*

Definitely
DOMINGUITA
★ Knight of the Cape ★

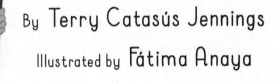

By Terry Catasús Jennings

Illustrated by Fátima Anaya

ALADDIN
New York London Toronto Sydney New Delhi

ALADDIN
An imprint of Simon & Schuster Children's Publishing Division
1230 Avenue of the Americas, New York, New York 10020
First Aladdin hardcover edition March 2021
Text copyright © 2021 by Terry Catasús Jennings
Jacket and title page illustrations copyright © 2021 by Mari Lobo
Interior illustrations copyright © 2021 by Fátima Anaya
Also available in an Aladdin paperback edition.
All rights reserved, including the right of reproduction in whole or in part in any form.
ALADDIN and related logo are registered trademarks of Simon & Schuster, Inc.
For information about special discounts for bulk purchases, please contact Simon & Schuster Special Sales at 1-866-506-1949 or business@simonandschuster.com.
The Simon & Schuster Speakers Bureau can bring authors to your live event. For more information or to book an event contact the Simon & Schuster Speakers Bureau at 1-866-248-3049 or visit our website at www.simonspeakers.com.
Book designed by Heather Palisi
The illustrations for this book were rendered digitally.
The text of this book was set in Candida.
Manufactured in the United States of America 0421 FFG
2 4 6 8 10 9 7 5 3
Library of Congress Control Number 2020948867
ISBN 9781534465039 (hc)
ISBN 9781534465022 (pbk)
ISBN 9781534465046 (ebook)

To Lou, who takes on the world so I can write
—T. C. J.

To my nephew, Memito, and my niece Sofi
—F. A.

Contents

1
A Dare

All Dominguita Melendez wanted to do today was read.

Her teacher, Mrs. Kannerpin, had encouraged her to "socialize" during recess. But Dominguita didn't want to socialize. She always had adventures to go on and new characters to meet. She ought to be able to read, right? Other kids got stars for reading *one* book, after all. And today, more than any other day, Dominguita just wanted to read.

It didn't look like she would be able to do what she wanted, though. Not with Ernie Bublassi heading her way.

"Krankypants wants you to join the game," he said.

Why couldn't Mrs. Kannerpin leave her alone? And why had she sent the biggest jerk in her grade to find her?

"She said someone needed to look for you, and I volunteered," Ernie said.

Great. He could read her mind.

"She wants you to come play dodgeball."

"Ugh." Dominguita slammed her book shut.

Ernie shrugged. "Everybody knows you read 'cause you don't have any friends."

"Huh? I do so have friends!" Dominguita's fists clenched.

"Who?"

She wanted to tell Ernie Bublassi the names of all her friends, but since Miranda moved to a place called Pascagoula in second grade, she'd been too busy reading to find any more friends.

"I don't need friends," she said, even though she still missed Miranda. "I'm studying to be a knight."

The minute she said it, she knew she was in trouble. *BIG trouble.* And it was all because Ernie Bublassi knew how to make her mad. And angry. And upset. And furious.

He grabbed her book. "A knight! *You* studying to be a knight? Girls can't be knights! I never heard of any girl-knights."

Dominguita would gladly have told him about Joan of Arc—she was a kind of knight, right? There must have been others. Dominguita was sure. But there was only one thing on her mind.

"Give it back! That's my grandmother's book!"

"Oh yeah? You studying to be an old-lady knight?" Ernie Bublassi threw the book in the playground dirt. "You'll never be a knight."

"I can *too* be a knight. I'll show you! And you are the meanest person in the universe!"

She picked the book up as if it were holy. And it was. It was one of the things her grandmother loved best, and right now Dominguita couldn't think of anything she loved more. She stomped toward the dodgeball game. It was the only way she would get rid of Ernie Bublassi.

But Ernie Bublassi wasn't through with her.

"Hey, guys!" he yelled as they reached the dodgeball game. "Dominguita's gonna be a knight. She's studying for it. A girl-knight. As if she wasn't weird enough already."

2
A Problem

It was a problem. A real problem. The truth was, Dominguita did not really want to be a knight. All she wanted to do right now was read the books she and Abuela used to read before bedtime. Starting with the one she'd been reading during recess—*Don Quijote*—Abuela's favorite. She needed to be reading to stay close to Abuela.

Because Abuela had left yesterday for Florida, to live with her sister.

Because Abuela couldn't remember things like she used to, and Dominguita's mami was afraid something would happen to her, alone, in their apartment, during the day.

Dominguita had begged. She promised to stay home after school every day so that Abuela didn't have to move away yet. Maybe she'd get better and she wouldn't have to go live with her sister at all!

Mami didn't think that would happen, so Abuela had to leave.

Dominguita missed Abuela worse than awful. Reading the books they used to read together helped make her feel like Abuela was still there. Just a little. They were books Abuela brought from Cuba. Kids' books about knights and pirates and travels around the world and under the sea.

But walking home, Dominguita did nothing but think about Ernie Bublassi. She planned and unplanned. Her brain spun. Her hands whirled and she talked to herself. She hated that Ernie was right. She didn't really have any friends. Not since Miranda. But there was nothing she could do about that. Maybe she could show him that she could be a knight. A knight like Don Quijote. She knew what Abuela would tell her: "You can even fight a giant if you set your mind to it."

She would show Ernie Bublassi what was what. She was not weird. And she could totally be a worthy knight!

How to be a knight was not a problem. She'd just about memorized *Don Quijote*. She knew King Arthur and his roundtable backward and forward.

The problem was how to prove it.

She needed her brother Rafi's help. Rafi used to be close to her, but not now.

Not now that he was in high school.

And he decided to play football and write for the school newspaper.

Before that, he played Parcheesi and Clue and Monopoly with her. Sometimes he would even join Abuela and Dominguita while they read aloud before bed. And he would tell Dominguita what books she might like and then they'd talk about them.

But now he was always practicing his tackles.

Or writing.

He never had time for Dominguita.

Except sometimes he tackled her just to practice.

Dominguita missed playing with her brother, but now she really needed him.

She leaned on the door to his room. "I'm gonna be a knight," she told him. "Starting now. And I need you to write a book about me."

Rafi's eyes narrowed. "And why do I need to write a book about you?"

This was the part she'd spent the most time thinking about. She wanted Rafi's help. She wanted Rafi to tell her she could beat Ernie Bublassi. She missed spending time with him. But what if Rafi was too busy? What if he didn't want to spend time helping her? She thought and thought, trying to figure out a way that she could hook him. It wasn't the reason at first, but once the idea of the book came to her . . . well . . . it was perfect.

"It's for Abuela," she said. "It's to help her. Like

she can still be with us. You know how we would always read at night? Before she left for Florida? Now she'll read the book about me. What could be better, right? We'll FaceTime with her every night. And then e-mail it to her. She can even tell her new friends about it. Give her something to talk about."

"Hmm. If she can remember."

"Exactly! She needs to have a book to remind her of what I did."

Rafi hadn't kicked her out of his room yet. Maybe it was working.

Dominguita kept going. She was counting on what was coming next. "That's not all. Ernie Bublassi said girls can't be knights. I have to prove him wrong."

"Wait." Rafi sat straight up. "Did you say Bublassi? One of the dastardly Bublassi brothers? The biggest bullies in Mundytown?"

Dominguita nodded solemnly. "Yup. The third-grade Bublassi."

"You're not friends with him, are you?"

"No way!"

Dominguita told her brother what had happened. "He can't get away with saying that girls can't be knights," she told him, then lowered her voice. "And he said I was weird."

"No!"

Dominguita nodded.

"Holy cow! You definitely have to show him." Dominguita had Rafi's attention now. "Rico Bublassi's in my grade and he's the biggest jerk ever. I love this!"

She had him! He was going to help her!

But he sat back down.

"Any Bublassi I know won't read a book."

He had her there. But she had already figured that out too.

She pulled out her phone. "Remember? Mami gave me a phone since Abuela's not here. It's so I can call her at work if I'm abducted by aliens or she needs to know I'm home."

Rafi gave one very slow nod.

"So whenever I do something knightly, I'll take a selfie. I can't just hand Ernie a bunch of selfies, right?" Dominguita could see the wheels turning in her brother's head. She took a breath and barreled on. "So we make a book. A book of pictures of my knightly adventures. He'll look at that. Especially if we have lots of pictures. Of course they'll have to be heroic."

"Heroic, yes. And lots of them, yes. I think you've got it. I think it will work. We'll show those Bublassi brothers what's what. I'll definitely help you!"

Rafi sprang to his closet and rummaged on the floor. "And I have something perfect for a knight." He pulled out a slick poncho—army green.

"A poncho?"

"We'll make it into a cape."

"A cape?"

"I found it in the trash outside the Army Navy Surplus. I was sure I could use it for something, and now here you are. It will protect you. Don Quijote called himself the Knight of the Sad Face, right?"

Dominguita had no idea where her brother was going with that, but she nodded with enthusiasm.

"You will be El Caballero del Capote," Rafi said. "Get it? Cape/capote? You'll be the Knight of the Cape."

Dominguita grinned. It had worked! Rafi would help her become a knight. *And* they were finally spending time together again.

They cut off the bottom of the poncho so it wouldn't drag on the ground. They fixed one of the tattered ties at the neck with duct tape. She decided to keep the hood in case it rained.

Rafi admired his work. He nodded. "A most fearsome knight."

"And you'll write about me? Songs and poems like Don Quijote?"

"About your noble deeds with valiant steeds and rescues of damsels in distress!"

"I'll have to think about the whole damsels in distress part," Dominguita said.

"I get it." Rafi nodded. "When you tell me your

brave deeds and give me your pictures, I'll make a book. We'll show the Bublassi Bullies!"

"And send it to Abuela!" Dominguita gave her brother a high five. "I will tell you my deeds," she said. "When I've done them."

Now she had to convince her parents.

A Knight in Training

"I'm gonna be a knight," Dom said at dinner.

"A knight?" Papi said. "Will you fight dragons?"

"A knight!" Mami didn't give Dom a chance to answer her father. "You mean you'll be playing with friends?"

She wanted to answer Papi, but she really didn't know what to say. There were no dragons in Mundytown. And then Mami. Why did she always want her to have friends? Had Mami been talking to Mrs. Kannerpin? Sure, it would be nice, but why did *everyone* want her to have friends all of a sudden?

"No." Dom's voice was small when she said that.

"Oh," Mami said.

Dom needed her mother to be more excited. "Rafi's going to write a book about me. And we'll share it with Abuela. That way she'll have something to talk about with her new friends. Won't that be nice?"

"Ay, mi amor, Rafi, what a sweet idea! Abuela will totally love that."

"It'll be great!" Rafi said. "And she'll show . . ."

Dom kicked her brother under the table. She wasn't sure she wanted Mami and Papi to know about Ernie Bublassi.

But it was too late.

"What?" both her parents said at the same time.

Dom shook her head. "Ernie Bublassi said I couldn't be a knight. Girls can't be knights—that's what he says."

Papi jumped right in. "You'll have to show him, won't you!"

Dom waited. Mami could stop everything right here and right now. But she didn't!

"That Ernie Double Bubble doesn't know what he's talking about! You'll be a perfect knight. In fact, you'll be more than perfect. With all the reading you've done about knights, you'll be stupendous. A book. With pictures. That's exactly what you need," Mami declared.

Phew!!!

"I need to find armor. And a helmet. And a lance wouldn't be bad either."

"Mmm." Papi smoothed the scraggly hairs that sprouted from his chin. "I can help you with the lance. We'll go to the storage unit after dinner."

"And it's this weekend you're being a knight, right?" Mami asked.

"Yep. Starting in the morning."

"The weather's supposed to still be warm, so you won't need a coat. Just make sure you make your bed before you leave on your adventures."

It couldn't have worked out better. Mami wasn't even thinking about friends anymore.

★ ★ ★

On Saturday morning, Dom started out with her lance and Rafi's cape. The cape was perfect. The lance Papi found her was the other half of a closet pole. Lightweight metal. Just the right size for her to hold and even twirl around.

She'd made it perfect by adding the pointy end of Mami's turkey baster to it.

With duct tape.

She couldn't be happier.

Now, to look for adventure. At least for someone she could help. Wasn't that what knights did? At least when there weren't any dragons around?

Dominguita's home was on the sixth floor of an apartment building surrounded by other apartment buildings. The sun didn't peek onto the streets until high noon. Neighbors met on the stairs. They talked to one another from tiny balconies with rusty wrought-iron railings. They hung out on even rustier fire escapes. The streets were covered in cracked asphalt and potholes.

But to Dominguita this was the best place in the world. She knew all the streets and she knew all the shopkeepers. This was where she felt at home.

She took a right out of her building toward Eighteenth Street.

She walked for about three blocks. Looking. Looking. Looking. She saw people. And dogs. And a couple of cats. But no one needed her help. She wanted to find a spectacular adventure. An Ernie Bublassi kind of spectacular adventure.

But she wouldn't turn down any chances to be helpful. Knights helped anyone in need.

She finally found a lady, about as old as her Abuela, pulling a rolling cart with a couple of bags of groceries in it. It wouldn't be heroic, but at least she'd have someone to help. The woman was going in her direction.

Dom bowed low. "May I help you, kind lady?"

The woman looked at Dom sideways.

"I'm a knight," Dom explained. "I'm just doing kind deeds while I look for adventure."

"Oh."

"May I help you with your cart?"

"Uh . . ."

"I'm a knight. I'm doing kind deeds. And I'm going your way."

The woman finally nodded. "A knight! Well, of course you can help me. I live three blocks from here."

Dom pulled the woman's cart. For six blocks. Not three. The woman lost her way because she was talking. Then Dom carried the bags up three flights of steps. Not all at once. She took breaks at each

floor. Then she brought up the little rolling cart, too.

"I normally call my neighbor to help me up the steps," the woman said. "Thank you!"

Dom shook her head. "Knights are happy to help anyone in need."

As she walked down the steps from the woman's apartment, she knew that Ernie Bublassi wouldn't think helping an old lady carry her groceries was heroic. And maybe she wouldn't be able to tell Abuela, either. It might make her grandmother miss Mundytown. She used to carry her groceries home in a cart just like the woman Dom had helped.

Thinking of Abuela made Dom miss her again.

Abuela had always been there when she got home from school. When she had a funny joke to tell. When she had a problem she couldn't figure out. She needed to talk to Abuela right then.

She punched Abuela's number in her just-in-case-of-alien-invasion phone. Missing her grandmother was a good enough reason to use it.

"I'm going to be a knight," she told Abuela instead of saying how much she missed her.

"A knight, Dominguita? Like Don Quijote?"

"Yup. Just like him."

"And you have a helmet and a breastplate and all that?"

Dominguita told her about Rafi's cape and Papi's lance with the turkey baster on its end.

"I love it!" Abuela said. "You know my friend Emilio Fuentes? He has that salvage yard on Twenty-Fourth and Washington. I bet you could find the rest of your armor there. It's a junk shop."

"Hmm." One good thing about helping the lady was that Dom was now close to Twenty-Fourth and Washington. "Great idea!"

"Tell Emilio hello for me. I miss him."

Dom didn't want to talk about missing, so she changed the subject.

"And Rafi's gonna write a book about me. To send to you. So you can share it with your friends."

"Couldn't be more perfect," Abuela said. "Rafi, that friend of yours . . ."

Dom waited a minute. Her heart felt a big squeeze. Abuela had remembered el Señor Fuentes,

22

but she couldn't remember who her grandson was. "Rafi, remember? That's my brother. Your other grandkid."

"Yes, Rafi, of course! He's a good writer. I can't wait to see the book."

Dom saw Fuentes Salvage across the street. She told her grandmother. "I'll FaceTime with you tonight," she said. "And I'll tell you my adventures."

★ ★ ★

El Señor Fuentes had one blue eye and one brown eye. He sold things he got from places that people tore down. Abuela was right. If there was anywhere to find armor in her neighborhood, it would be at Fuentes Salvage.

"I'm about to become a knight," she told el Señor Fuentes. "I need some armor."

"A knight, Dominguita?" El Señor Fuentes raised the eyebrow over the blue eye.

That was the second time someone had said "A knight, Dominguita." It didn't sound quite right.

Not for a knight. Dominguita meant "little Sunday." How many fearsome knights were named after a day of the week?

"Dom," she said. That would be better.

The old man pursed his lips. "I see, Dom. But you were named after your grandmother."

"I know," Dom said. "She said to say 'hi.'"

El Señor Fuentes waited for a long second. "Still, Dom is a strong name for a knight. Dom inspires . . . respect."

"Just so." Dom's words came out of a corner of her brain. She was sure she'd read them in some knight book.

"What do you have in mind?"

"Any helmets lying around, or breastplates?"

"Hmmm. A helmet is very important." El Señor Fuentes slipped through the door behind his counter and came back with a small metal pail. "Perhaps this would do. I use it to water my plants."

Dom placed the little pail on her head. It didn't have a visor. Or a pointy top. It wasn't beautiful. Or scary. But the pail had enough room for her pigtails. And it fit. Her head would be safe. The handle would help it stay on.

"Thanks. How 'bout a breastplate? Any ideas?"

El Señor Fuentes took her around the shop.

It was like being at the three bears' house. Some pieces were too big. Others were too heavy. After a lot of looking, she found a piece that might be just right.

"A pet door!" El Señor Fuentes exclaimed.

Dom tried it on for size. "It fits!"

El Señor Fuentes threaded two leather shoelaces through the screw holes on the pet door. "Voilà. Arm straps! A perfect breastplate for a daring knight."

Dom grinned. She posed, her arms spreading out the cape.

"I'm the Knight of the Cape—Dom del Capote."

"A worthy name."

"Worthy."

The old man nodded several times, but then he raised the eyebrow over his brown eye. "Why not just Dom Capote? Don Quijote . . . Dom Capote?"

"YES!" She loved the ring of it.

"Dom Capote, the Knight of the Cape."

Dom nodded. "Just so." Saying that now felt right.

She caught her image on a piece of broken glass leaning against the wall. No one would think she was Don Quijote, especially not Ernie Bublassi. But it wasn't bad, either. And it didn't matter what she looked like. Her deeds would speak louder than her looks.

She fixed the helmet on her head. She straightened her breastplate. She tugged on her cape to make it sit right on her shoulders, and she asked el Señor Fuentes to take her picture.

"You look most wonderful, Good Knight," el Señor Fuentes said, handing her phone back.

Dom was about to turn toward the door, but the words stopped her.

"What's wrong, Dominguita . . . Dom?"

"Ah, well." Dom's voice was not as sure as before. "I . . . I . . . I'm not a knight. Not yet. I need someone to knight me!"

El Señor Fuentes scrunched his forehead. He

pursed his lips. His blue eye and his brown eye darted back and forth as if trying to find the answer on the counter in front of him. "Yes. You need someone with a sword. That might be hard to find in Mundytown."

For a few seconds, neither one of them spoke.

"Perhaps you can find a sword tomorrow, you know? For now you can be a knight-in-training. And you can still do knightly deeds."

"A knight-in-training! Yes! Anything you need? I'm here. Happy to help with a knightly deed," Dom said.

The junk shop owner shook his head. "Nothing heroic," he said.

"Anything," Dom said.

El Señor Fuentes reached for a bag. "Well, you could deliver this to my granddaughter. We live three blocks away. She needs it, and if I take it, I'll have to close the shop."

"Happy to do it. Knights are always willing to help."

El Señor Fuentes's granddaughter, Leni, was so happy Dom had helped her grandfather that she gave Dom a hug.

She could count the delivery in her knightly deeds even though she wasn't a knight yet, but it wasn't good enough for Ernie Bublassi.

Dom walked one more block. Her stomach began to make noises. Maybe it was because she'd walked a lot already this morning, or maybe it was because of the smell that surrounded her.

She followed her nose a short distance to Yuca, Yuca, the best Cuban restaurant in the universe. It was also the only Cuban restaurant in Mundytown, but that was beside the point. The thing was, Cuban food would make her feel closer to Abuela. And that would make her feel good right now.

4
A Squire

Dom and her family visited Yuca, Yuca often. She liked el Señor Prieto, the owner. And she loved his food.

"And what have we here?" el Señor Prieto asked when Dom strutted in.

"I'm a knight-errant, Señor Prieto. I walk around and do good deeds, and I'd like some black beans and plantains." She said it as if she had a right to say it. A knight would never plead for food, but she decided to add "Please." Knights should always be polite.

"My pleasure, O wondrous knight." El Señor Prieto spooned black beans and plantains onto a plate. "Yuca fritters?"

"Please." It wouldn't do to turn down a castellan when he was offering a feast.

"Where will you be going?"

"Here and there," she said through a mouthful of beans. "Looking for adventure. I already helped a lady with her groceries. And I did an errand for el Señor Fuentes." She decided to keep the book for Abuela and Ernie Bublassi's dare to herself.

"Ah, adventure." El Señor Prieto wiped the counter as he talked to Dom. He stopped and scratched his beard. "I suspect you'll find plenty around here. Just yesterday, I heard there was a damsel in distress. Her foot got caught in a sewer grate."

"Did she get it out?"

"Yes, she did. But no knight helped her, if that's what you're asking."

"Mmm." Dom held up a finger while she swallowed the plantain in her mouth. She had made a decision on the damsel thing. "Most damsels can take care of themselves. I'm going to rescue *anyone* who's in distress. Not just damsels."

El Señor Prieto nodded. "I understand, of course."

Dom ate in silence for a few more bites. She reached for another fritter.

"Thank you for providing this feast. Most castellans will do the same . . . in my travels, that is."

"Providing a feast? Hmmm. I wonder if other castellans would feed you without asking for. . . you know . . . some . . . compensation?"

"Com-pen-sation?"

"Money," el Señor Prieto said as if the word hurt his mouth.

"Money?" Dom almost choked on the yuca fritter. Don Quijote had expected to be fed in the castles he visited. Still, el Señor Prieto could be right.

"Many castellans will want to be paid when they feed you," he said. "A knight should always be prepared."

Dom thought about it. She had a little bit of money in her piggy bank. Very little. It wouldn't last the weekend. She needed to earn some money.

"Do you have a job I can do, Señor Prieto?"

"You mean to earn money for food?"

Dom nodded.

"I could use someone to sweep the sidewalk in the morning. In the evening, too." El Señor Prieto kept thinking. "How about this? If you sweep my sidewalk in the mornings and in the evenings, while you're on your adventures, I'll provide your lunch. That should keep you fed during your quest."

"Just so." The new knight stepped down from the stool.

"Forgive me for getting in your business, kind knight, but do you have a squire, like Sancho Panza? Someone to keep you company? To carry your saddlebags?"

"Saddlebags?"

El Señor Prieto pulled out a backpack-looking thing from behind the counter. "This will make an excellent saddlebag," he said. "You can use it to keep an extra shirt. And it will keep your lunch warm. You should also take water. Your squire

could carry it. I know just the man. . . . Pancho," el Señor Prieto called back toward the kitchen. Then he turned back to Dom. "My nephew will be glad to help you."

Oh no! Dom was doomed. Pancho Sanchez was the chickenest of the chickens in third grade.

If danger ever came, Pancho fell over and played dead like a possum. Or he ran into the bushes and tried to camouflage himself like a chameleon.

Still. A knight couldn't turn away a kindness, and el Señor Prieto was offering to feed her. Besides, Pancho was big. For a coward, he was pretty smart. And el Señor Prieto was right. She needed someone to carry her saddlebag. It would leave her hands free for her lance. And Pancho could also record her deeds in pictures.

If she really thought about it, Pancho could be a good squire. He knew a lot about animals. Maybe he would be useful if they were attacked by a troop of monkeys, a pride of lions, or a crash of rhinos.

"Hi, Pancho. I'm a knight-errant going on a quest. Wanna come?"

Pancho Sanchez didn't have anything better to do. Like Dom, he didn't have many friends. He agreed. Dom Capote sent him home to find some bottles of water and a first aid kit.

While Pancho was gone, Dom Capote swept the sidewalk in front of Yuca, Yuca, and then ran to her own home. She scraped out all the contents of her piggy bank and snatched a couple of T-shirts from the clean-laundry basket.

She tried to tell her brother about what she'd done so far. "What do you think?" she asked him after she finished.

"Great," he said, but he didn't take his eyes off his computer.

"Bublassi brothers, remember?"

Rafi nodded. "Yeah, yeah, go get 'em."

Ugh! Had he forgotten already?

She met Pancho Sanchez on the way back to Yuca, Yuca. They took a selfie together and set off on their quest.

5
A Steed

She was sure a new adventure would come to meet them. Soon. Something worthy of both Abuela and Ernie Bublassi. She didn't have to worry. After all, aren't people in need everywhere, all the time? It was still early.

Except today was a bad day for finding adventure. Dom Capote and her trusty squire searched the neighborhood. They cruised by the basketball court on Fifteenth Street. By the fire station on Twelfth.

Nothing. Dom was getting desperate. She had to do something knightly and prove Ernie Bublassi wrong. And she had to do it before Monday morning or Ernie Bublassi would have everyone in third grade laughing at her.

At Eighth Street, they found something.

It wasn't adventure and it came from behind a dumpster.

It was a mangy mutt, his stomach so bowed it almost touched the ground and his ears so long, they did. The mutt greeted them with a toothy smile.

"A steed!" Dom Capote pointed to the dog.

"A dog. A steed is something you can ride. Like a horse. You can't ride a dog."

"I don't have to ride him for him to be my steed. He could carry our saddlebag. And pull a cart if we ever find one."

Pancho Sanchez gave her a doubting look.

"Go on, let him carry our saddlebag."

"Huh?"

"The saddlebag!" Dom Capote commanded.

The startled Pancho did as he was told. He

fumbled to tie the saddlebag to the mutt's back. Whatever he did, the pack fell and hit the ground. The water bottles bounced out.

"I'll carry the saddlebag for now," Pancho said. He hoisted it back onto his shoulder.

Dom Capote had to agree. "Tomorrow we'll find a better saddlebag."

The mutt kept sniffing Pancho's pack, though. He sniffed and sniffed and nipped at its bottom.

"What do you have in there?"

Pancho looked sadder than if he'd lost his best friend. "Ham biscuits," he mumbled. "The ones my uncle sent."

"Share one with our trusty steed. That will make him want to go on the adventure with us."

Pancho handed the dog one of the ham biscuits. It was easy to tell what a bad idea he thought this was. How Dom was acting way more than crazy. How he wished they still had four biscuits instead of three.

"See," Dom Capote said. "He's totally grateful. Now he'll follow us forever."

It was true. The mutt's toothy grin was back. His tail wagged. With his belly still dangerously close to the ground, he followed Dom Capote and her squire.

"We'll call him Rocinante, like Don Quijote's horse."

"Roci-what?" Pancho asked. He flung the saddlebag on his shoulder again.

"Roh-see-NAN-teh! Roh-see-NAN-teh! Don't you remember?"

"Well, yeah. I remember it was something like that. But that's a really hard name." Pancho scrunched his forehead and made like he was calling the mutt. "Here, Roh-see-NAN-teh! Roh-see-NAN-teh!" He shook his head. "It will never work."

"Mmm."

"Why don't we call him Roco?"

"Roco." Dom did the sign of the cross over the dog. "I name you Roco."

Roco didn't seem to mind. The knight, her squire, and her steed walked on.

6
A Rescue That Was Not So Daring

"I hope our new steed will turn our luck." Dom Capote sighed. "We really need to find an adventure so my brother can write about it."

Pancho stopped. He dropped the saddlebag.

Dom stopped next to him. "What?"

"What'd you just say?"

"My brother. My brother. He's going to write a book about me." She decided she'd better be honest with Pancho, since he was her squire. "Ernie

Bublassi said girls can't be knights, and I'm going to prove him wrong. But I need to have some adventures first."

At the mention of Ernie Bublassi, Pancho straightened up. He looked at Dom as if this were the first time he'd seen her. "Is that why you're taking all the pictures?"

Dom nodded with importance.

"I'm in." Pancho started walking again. Not just walking. Strutting. Like he was really going somewhere.

Perhaps it was fate, or perhaps it was Roco, but in three more blocks the steed found adventure.

"Grrr!" He pounced on a bush.

A cat scurried out, with something in her mouth.

Roco, Dom, and Pancho chased it.

They cornered the cat against a wall.

"EEK! A bunny!"

Dom couldn't argue with that. A bunny dangled from the cat's mouth as if it were a kitten.

"You have to save it!" Pancho screamed.

"Me? You're the squire!"

"No, no, the knight always rescues whoever's in distress."

There was no way for Dom to argue with that, either. Besides, Pancho was lying on the grass curled up like a baby, shaking.

"Dom Capote to the rescue!" Dom roared. She pounced on the cat and wrapped it in her cape.

"You're mine now, you scoundrel!"

Dom had the cat, but she needed help to rescue the poor little bunny.

"Pancho Sanchez!"

"Ye-e-e-s, Dom?"

"Stop playing dead. I need your help."

Pancho got up and slowly headed toward the huddle of dog, Dom, cape, and cat as if he'd been called to the principal's office at school.

"Hold the cat!"

Pancho did as he was told. Through the cape.

Dom lifted a corner to find the petrified cat with the shivering bunny still in its mouth.

"Hmmm." Dom lifted her eyes to Pancho. "And what do I do now?"

"Open its mouth."

"You know all about animals. Why don't you?" But Dom already knew the answer.

Careful, careful, she told herself. She gripped the cat's top jaw with her left hand. Shaking, she pulled the bottom jaw open with her right. The bunny dropped. With one swift move, Dom caught it before it touched the ground.

Pancho let go of both the cape and cat. "Scram!"

The no-longer-petrified cat ran.

The bunny wiggled its soft pink ears. It winked at them. It was alive!

"You did it!" Pancho snapped pictures and jumped up and down.

Dom tried to look humble. That's what knights were supposed to do. Rescue whoever needed rescuing, right? Still, she was pleased. And she was tickled pink that Pancho took pictures without being asked.

Pancho turned the bunny 'round and 'round to see if it was hurt. "Poor baby! Look at that scratch! Let's take it to the shelter."

"Great idea, Pancho Sanchez, Squire!"

"We have to find the other bunnies. What if the cat comes back to the nest again?"

"You think? That cat will never want to tangle with the likes of us again! I'm sure we have nothing to worry about."

"Tell you what . . ." Pancho rummaged in the saddlebag. "Here's some stuff my mom uses when we get hurt. Let's spread it on those scratches after we clean them out. I'll put the bunny in my pocket and we'll find the others. We'll take them all to the shelter."

Dom had to admit that was a good idea. And she had been right; Pancho could take care of animals.

With the little bundle of fur in Pancho's pocket, Dom took the next step. She pointed. "Roco! Find the bunnies."

Roco did.

Close by, under a root, in a hollow in the dirt. Five more bunnies.

"I'll take three, you take the other two," said Dom.

"Let's leave them," said Pancho.

"You said we should take them to the shelter!"

Pancho pointed. The mother rabbit hid behind the bush, watching them.

"They'll be better off with their mother," he whispered.

"Why don't we take them all?"

"Why don't we leave them where they belong." Pancho took the bunny out of his pocket and slipped it into the nest.

"But the cat!"

"Didn't you say the cat would never want to tangle with the likes of us again?"

Dom thought. She nodded. "Just so."

They tiptoed away, looking back at the nest every few steps.

"Having adventures makes a squire hungry," Pancho said.

"A knight, too!"

Pancho plunged into the saddlebag and came up with three biscuits. One for Dom, one for Roco, and the last one for himself.

Dom hadn't even finished her biscuit when Roco stiffened and pointed. The cat! Again!

"Woewayway, you scoundwerel!" Dom yelled through her biscuit.

"The shelter!"

They carefully lay the bunnies in the saddlebag. Pancho left the top open so they could breathe. Dom and Roco cornered the mother. After a little struggle, Dom managed to cradle her in a sling made from her cape.

The animal shelter on Sixth Street welcomed them. The manager of the shelter praised the knight and her squire for their bravery.

"We'll put a flyer on our window," she said. "And put the word out in the neighborhood. She's not a field rabbit. She's somebody's pet for sure. Someone might be really grateful to you."

Dom glowed. Exactly what a knight-errant needed on her first quest.

Dom washed her hands in the hall bathroom and screeched into the dining room. Mami, Papi, and Rafi were all waiting.

"You're late, Dominguita," Mami said.

"Sorry, sorry, sorry. I was busy with an exciting rescue!"

"Tell me your deeds, brave knight," Rafi said. "How were your adventures?"

"Magnificent!" Dom served herself meat loaf and mashed potatoes. Not the Cuban food Abuela would have cooked, but still. It was good. She told the story of her day between bites.

"Bunnies?" Mami exclaimed. "Abuela will love it. You know how much she likes furry things."

"Oh yeah. She'll love it," Papi said, but Dom could tell he wasn't really excited.

Dom looked at her brother, but Rafi was deep in his mashed potatoes.

"The cat was scary," Dom said. "Just ask Pancho. He was quivering all over the place."

"Hmmm." Rafi stood up and cleared his plate from the table.

After the dishes were done, Dom FaceTimed Abuela and told her all about her day. She also told Abuela that Rafi wasn't impressed. And if Rafi wasn't impressed, he might not write the book.

"I think it was a good enough adventure," Abuela said. "I bet if you talk to him again, he'll change his mind. Besides, I want every little deed in the book."

"Right," Dom said. Abuela was right. Rafi would change his mind if Abuela said so. But it turned out not to be that easy.

"Look," her brother said. "What do you think Ernie Bublassi will say about bunnies?"

"Oh."

"Yeah. Oh."

"The people at the shelter thought we were brave. I sent them our picture to put in their newsletter."

"They're not Ernie Bublassi!"

"We-e-ell . . ." She was desperate to change her brother's mind. "Rescuing bunnies isn't as fearsome as fighting an army of knights on horseback, but it is something. Abuela wants you to write about it anyway. It wasn't a great adventure, but it was a good adventure. Good enough. I didn't have time to find an amazing adventure today. Tomorrow I'll do something better. Something worthy of a fearsome knight!"

"You'd better," Rafi said. "It's gonna take something really huge to show up Ernie Bublassi."

Dom shuffled off to the living room. She plopped on the couch and didn't even turn on the television. How could she become a fearsome and worthy knight?

"You know what you need to go along with the bunnies?" Rafi said, suddenly by her ear. "A knighting ceremony. You need someone to dub you a knight. *That* will amaze Ernie Bublassi. Then you can throw the bunnies in as a bonus. I know how we can do it."

"Now, why didn't I think of that? We'll need a sword—that's what el Señor Fuentes said. And someone to dub me."

"Mr. Kowalski has an awesome sword hanging right in his grocery store." Rafi had delivered groceries for Kowalski's the previous summer.

"And he's a nobleman?"

"It's a really awesome sword."

"Do you think he'll do it?"

"I'll call him right now."

★ ★ ★

"No worries," Rafi said when he got off the phone. "Mr. Kowalski comes from a most honorable line of knights in Poland. And he'll be happy to knight you."

"You think?"

"I told him Dom Capote, the Knight of the Cape, would soon be over."

And Rafi offered something even better. Since it might be dark, he'd take her there now and pick her up when she was done.

7
A Knighting Ceremony

Kowalski's Grocery was two blocks from Fuentes Salvage. Dom ran as fast as the pail on her head would let her—it kept slipping down on her nose and covering her eyes. When she reached the grocery store, Mr. Kowalski was waiting for her.

"Ah, Don Capote, the knight in shining armor!" Mr. Kowalski bowed. He had a bushy brown and black mustache, like the wooly worms that tell how long winter's going to last.

"Dom," she said. "Not Don. And I'm not a knight yet. That's what you're supposed to do."

"Ah yes. I see. My wife is already looking for the key to the sword case." He pointed to a glass case high on a wall, below a neon sign for Puckered Pickles.

Dom gasped. The case was bathed in light from the pickle sign. The silver blade gleamed neon green. It looked magical. Like it had been placed there just for her. A circle with a fancy *K* filled the middle of the sword's golden handle. Swirly lines surrounded it. Below the black leather sheath, a silky pom-pom hung like a pendulum from a clock. The perfect sword for a knighting ceremony.

"Where did it come from?" Dom asked, snapping a picture.

"My Polish ancestors. Handed down through generations," Mr. Kowalski said.

"Very suitable." Dom thought that's what a knight would say. Then she thought she'd better check that Rafi had been right.

"You come from a long line of knights?" she

53

asked. She didn't want to give Ernie Bublassi any reason to say she wasn't a knight.

"Knights and kings!" The woolly worm jumped as he talked. "Who else but noblemen would call such a handsome sword their own! We'll knight you as soon as my wife finds the key."

"Most honored," Dom said, starting to slip out of her armor. "You know, I need to hold a vigil over my armor before I can become a knight."

"Mmm."

"That's what all the knight books say. Don Quijote, King Arthur . . . they spent the night watching over their armor before they were dubbed."

"Mmmmmm."

Dom nodded, as if Mr. Kowalski had agreed. "I'll find a corner, by the vegetables. Nobody goes over there anyway."

"We close at nine o'clock. . . ."

"No problem. Rafi's coming by to pick me up at closing."

Dom carried her armor to the fruit and vegetable aisle. She had to step over a pineapple. And almost slipped on an orange. It wasn't a very orderly place. Mr. Kowalski must be too busy to keep it neat. Perhaps Dom could help since Mr. Kowalski had agreed to dub her with his awesome, noble sword. That's what a good knight would do.

Quickly, she arranged each fruit and vegetable bin. She made pyramids of pineapples. And rows of radishes. She lined up the limes and the lemons. And arranged the apples by type. She even read the number on the sticker to make sure she put the right ones together. Another good deed for a knight-to-be!

When she was done, Dom placed her armor between the bins of rutabagas and parsnips. She lay it down as if bringing a baby bird back to its nest.

Then she stood over it.

She stood on one leg. And then on the other. She knelt over the armor. She recited nursery rhymes and *The Night Before Christmas*. She sang the songs her mami sang to her when she was little. She sneaked a peek at the clock. *What?* Only forty minutes had passed since her vigil had started.

She paced up and down the vegetable aisle one more time and then decided it was time to get dubbed. She bundled up her armor and stepped toward the register.

"I think my vigil has lasted long enough," she said as soon as Mr. Kowalski was free. "You can dub me any time you're ready."

"But I thought you were staying till nine!"

Dom shrugged. "Don Quijote didn't last very long, either. We should go ahead. I called Rafi. He's on his way over."

She put on her armor, knelt, and bowed her head.

"Uh . . . Dom . . . my wife hasn't found the key to the sword case yet."

"Oh."

"Yeah . . ."

"We'll have to make do."

"What about this?" Mr. Kowalski showed her a stick he used to bring down the metal shutters that protected the store at night. It ended in a hook.

Dom used a corner of her cape to wipe the grease off the end.

"It'll work," she said. "But since your wife isn't here, let's wait for Rafi. He can take a picture."

"Of course," Mr. Kowalski said.

★ ★ ★

"The sword's locked up," she told her brother when he got there. "You think that'll be a problem?"

"Never!" Rafi said. "I'll take a picture of the sword and photoshop it in. It's a little cheat, but it's to put Ernie Bublassi in his place. No problem."

Dom knelt again in front of Mr. Kowalski.

He raised the stick. "By the power vested in me by . . ." Mr. Kowalski looked around for whoever should have vested the power in him.

Dom shrugged and motioned for him to go on.

"By the power vested in me, I dub you Sir Dom Capote, the Knight of the Cape." Mr. Kowalski

touched the stick to each of Dom's shoulders. The phone flashed.

Dom stayed down as if in silent prayer. Something should be happening, right? Some kind of feeling? But there was none.

"Picture came out great," Rafi said, trying to break the awkward moment.

"Yes, you may rise," Mr. Kowalski said.

"Thank you, my good man," Dom told the grocer.

"Best of luck to you, Dom Capote."

"Okay," she told her brother. "I did another good deed, but you don't have to say anything about it. I was glad to do it for Mr. Kowalski. So when you do the book, just a little bit on the bunnies and a lot on the knighting. Put the pictures all around it. Ernie will want to know that I was dubbed properly."

"As you wish, great knight."

8
A Bully

The next day, before the sun cracked the tops of the apartment buildings, Dom perched on the fire escape throwing pebbles at Pancho Sanchez's window. Roco barked from the sidewalk. Dom had brought him a blanket and a cereal bowl full of water the night before, and he'd stayed right by the door to her building. She'd give him some breakfast from Yuca, Yuca.

Roco's bark and the pebbles did their jobs. A

sleepy Pancho opened the window. The mop of black hair on his head hadn't made up its mind what to do yet.

"If you want to be a squire," Dom said, "you'd better be up early."

"Why would I get up early on a Sunday!"

"We're on a quest! We need to find a really good adventure." Dom pivoted, like a soldier. "I'll see you at Yuca, Yuca in twenty minutes. Be there!"

"Ugh!"

★ ★ ★

El Señor Prieto waved a dishcloth as Dom stepped into the restaurant. "Tell me about your quest yesterday, O wondrous knight."

Dom shrugged "We rescued some bunnies from a cat."

"You sound disappointed."

This time she explained about Ernie Bublassi and needing the pictures. And the book. "Rafi didn't think it was a great adventure. Or my papi. I don't think Pancho did, either. Not for proving I'm a great and fearsome girl-knight. Abuela said we should count everything, but she loves me, you know?"

Pancho's uncle held himself straight up as if Pancho and Rafi had challenged him to a duel. He scratched his beard in deep thought. "I'm sure she meant it. And she was proud of your deeds! Tell me every detail. I'll tell you if it was suitable for a knight."

Dom did.

El Señor Prieto was very impressed. "Well, then," he said. "Would Don Quijote be disappointed at such an adventure?"

Dom reached for the broom. How would Don Quijote feel? What would Don Quijote do?

She straightened her shoulders, shouldered the broom, and headed out the door. She nodded, mostly at herself. "He would say what I told Rafi last night. Today. Today we'll have a real adventure."

By the time Pancho got there, Dom was munching on buñuelos. A plateful of the figure-eight pastries bathed in sticky syrup lay on the counter. Pancho's eyes bugged out.

"Hola, Tío," Pancho Sanchez said. "Can I . . . ?"

"Time to go!" Dom stuffed a last bite into her mouth. She licked her fingers and grabbed the bag el Señor Prieto had made for their lunch. "I was dubbed last night. I'm a real knight now and we're having a *real* adventure today, Pancho. Gotta get started."

"But . . . but . . ."

"Here you go, Pancho." El Señor Prieto wrapped a buñuelo in a napkin for his nephew.

Pancho grabbed the gift from his uncle and stuck his tongue out at Dom's back. He munched as they left Yuca, Yuca. He even shared a bite with Roco.

The knight, her squire, and the steed walked in the opposite direction from the day before.

Dom told Pancho about the knighting ceremony. "My brother put our pictures into a book last night.

And he wrote down all our adventures." Dom didn't tell Pancho that Rafi thought their bunny adventure was too lame to impress Ernie Bublassi. "He said he and I would be like Miguel de Cervantes and Don Quijote."

"Umph." Pancho licked his fingers as they walked.

"And your uncle said we were most"—Dom scanned a far corner of her mind—"most IN-tre-pid!"

"My mom said don't be late for dinner again."

They looked for adventure. Heroic adventure. Adventure that Rafi would want to write about. With pictures that would blow Ernie Bublassi's socks off.

Roco helped. He smelled everything along the way.

Dom Capote checked every cross street. She peeked up. Maybe she could find mischief in high places. They walked for blocks.

Pancho grumbled. And grumbled. Until he saw a fountain.

A girl about their age sat on its edge, dangling her legs in the water.

Roco leaped forward to take a drink.

"That fountain looks cool," Pancho said.

"Don't even think about it. We're on a quest!"

"Can't we just stop our quest for a bit to cool down?"

Dom wanted to tell Pancho what she thought about his whining, but a blur passed by the corner of her eye.

"Hey!" the girl on the fountain shrieked. "Gimme back my brace!"

Dom took off after a curly headed boy carrying a black metal and foam thing in his hand.

The boy was fast, but Dom was faster. She cornered him against a hedge.

"What are you doing, villain?" Dom faced the curly headed boy, lance in hand.

The bully turned and sneered. "What does it look like I'm doing, buckethead?"

Dom pointed the lance. "Give that leg brace back."

"Says who?"

"I am Dom Capote, a knight-errant." She swept her lance back toward Pancho. "This is my squire."

"You're an error, that's for sure."

"Errant. Errant. Knight-errant." Dom stomped her foot. "That means I wander around looking for adventure and for creatures who need rescuing."

"Yeah, right." The bully wasn't giving up the brace. "Why don't you rescue your squire, there. He's hiding in the bushes."

Dom looked. The curly haired boy was right. A mop of black hair sticking out from a bush behind her was the only sign of her squire. Dom threw up her arms. "PANCHO!"

She didn't really mean to do it, but as her hands, coiled tight around her lance, rose, the lance caught the leg brace. Score! Now that she had the prize, Dom yanked hard. The brace jerked out of the curly headed boy's hands and flew back toward the fountain. In one swift, and totally awkward, motion.

"Whoa, whoa, buckethead. I didn't do nothin'."

"I didn't do *anything*." There were few things Dom liked less than incorrectly used double negatives.

"Yes, you did," the girl yelled from the fountain. "You got my brace back."

9
A Knight's Trust

Dom concentrated on the bully in front of her. Should she teach him a lesson, or should she be kind? Perhaps she should be more than kind. The girl had told the truth. Dom had gotten the brace back. She had won. And after all, if she was trying to be a knight, she should act like a knight.

Menacing, Dom lowered her voice. "I should tattle on you," she said. "But I will trust your honor as a gentleman. Promise never to bother this girl again. Actually . . ." Dom decided she'd really make it good. "Promise never to bother anyone again. If you promise, I will let you go."

The bully seemed stunned for a second. Then his eyes widened and he grinned. Pancho, on the other hand, lunged to Dom's side.

"What are you doing?" Pancho yelled. "Trust? Honor? What are you talking about? That's Ernie's brother Ponsi!"

"Quiet, Squire! I will trust him if he promises." Dom stared at Ponsi. "Ponsi Bublassi, do you promise?"

A crooked smile snaked across the bully's face. He nodded. "I promise to be kind to all. I promise to hurt no one, O error-knight. Trust me, you can." The boy ended with a loud snort.

"Well, then." This had been a lot easier than Dom Capote had expected. "Go in peace."

"You as well, error-night." Ponsi bowed to the ground, smirking all the way.

"How 'bout that smile?" Dom punched Pancho as the boy disappeared around the hedge. "Did you hear the happiness in his voice? He's changed his ways."

"Oh sure," Pancho grumbled, shuffling behind her. "The bully of fifth grade turned into a saint. Didn't you hear what I said? That's Ponsi Bublassi! Next in line of the Bublassi brothers!"

Dom's heart stopped for a second. Was Pancho right? This was Ernie Bublassi's brother? A smile crept onto her face. She had beaten Ernie Bublassi's brother! SHE HAD BEATEN ERNIE BUBLASSI'S BROTHER! She set her jaw, handed Pancho her phone, and marched toward the fountain.

"Let's talk to the girl we rescued. I'm sure she's grateful."

"I hate it when the Bublassi brothers pick on girls."

That stopped Dom. "Pancho," she said. "I did not rescue her because she's a girl. I rescued her because she was being bullied. Normally, girls can take care of themselves. Got it?"

Pancho stared and nodded slowly.

"And we need to get a picture for the Ernie-Bublassi-I'll-show-you book. We need to find out her name."

Pancho shrugged. "Her name is Steph," he said. "She had an operation. That's why she needs the brace. Let's walk her home. What if Ponsi comes back?"

Dom could see this was going to be difficult. Pancho still thought that girls needed protecting, and he didn't understand the finer points of being a knight. "No, no," she said. "You're wrong. I'm sure Ponsi will never hurt anyone again. He gave me his word."

Pancho's jaw dropped. He stared hard at Dom for a few seconds.

"We need to take her home." Pancho was quiet but firm.

Dom shook her head again. They had almost reached Steph.

"Thanks," Steph said as they approached. "That kid's always after me. Calling me names. I was just sitting here and he ran away with my brace."

"Don't thank me," Pancho said. "The honor is all Dom's. She did it all."

"Are you playing knights?" Steph asked.

"Playing?" Pancho said. "She's a real knight. Dom Capote. Doer of brave deeds." Pancho pointed to the dog. "And this is her steed, Roco. I'm just her squire. We are on a quest to prove girls can be knights. Let me take your picture to record this adventure."

Dom tried to smile and look heroic at the same time. She liked what Pancho was saying, but it didn't feel right. Not for Pancho. Not the way he'd been talking just minutes before. Wait, what was he trying to do?

Pancho took the picture and babbled on. "Perhaps we should stop for a bite to celebrate Dom's brave deeds," he told Steph. "And you can celebrate with us."

Dom was still confused, but she liked Pancho's idea. "A brilliant idea, Squire. A brilliant idea!"

Dom used her piggy bank money to buy some drinks from a food truck. They sat against the base of a statue of a dead general.

Pancho opened the saddlebag and pulled out the ham croquettes his uncle had given them for their lunch that morning. He sighed. Instead of two each, they could now only have one each. The fourth one was for Roco.

"He won't leave me alone," Steph said between bites. "He keeps hanging around. I don't know what he wants with me."

"Dom is sure he won't bother you again," said Pancho. His eyebrows almost reached the mop of black hair on his head.

Dom jumped at Pancho's words. "He gave me his word as a gentleman. There's nothing to worry about."

Pancho looked at Dom in front of him. "I know what you're thinking," he said. "You're thinking this is like Don Quijote. But it's not. Ponsi Bublassi will never give up."

"Not so!" Dom said.

Pancho leaned close to Dom and spoke softly. "We need to take her home. That way her family can thank you properly. They might even tell the world about your noble deeds."

Now that was a good idea! Maybe Pancho was beginning to understand the knightly ways. And even if she hadn't convinced him, if Steph's family recognized her daring deeds, Pancho would have to believe.

She smiled. "Just so, Pancho. Just so."

An Unexpected Addition

Steph lived in a house with a porch full of flowers: drooping flowers, shooting flowers, trailing flowers, dead flowers. A white-haired woman dressed in lavender opened the door. She smiled when she saw Steph with Dom and Pancho.

"You brought friends!"

The knight shook her head. "Well, no, not really."

"Yes." Pancho followed his nose inside the house. "We're Steph's friends. We brought her home."

Dang. Dom wished Pancho had kept his mouth shut. She didn't want Steph's grandmother to get the wrong idea. She had rescued Steph, but they weren't friends. She kind of liked having Pancho as a friend. And it wouldn't be bad if she had another friend. But Don Quijote only had a squire. And she couldn't become friends with everyone she rescued, could she?

"I'm so happy to see you." Steph's grandmother held the door open wide. "Here, here, come in. I was so afraid when she came to stay with me that Steph would be lonely. I just took cookies out of the oven. Would you like some?"

"We must be going." Dom backed away from the door. "We're—"

"Sort of in a hurry," Pancho finished. "But we have enough time for cookies."

Dom pouted, her forehead wrinkled, and her eyes became slits.

"A feast, remember? To celebrate your feats. So they can tell everyone about your noble deeds."

"Uh . . ."

Steph stepped in. "Grandma, this is Dom. She's a knight. And this is Pancho—he's her squire. They rescued me from that kid."

"I see." The grandmother tried to smile but didn't do a very good job.

"I can't stay inside all the time, Grandma." Steph patted her grandmother's arm. "And I'm supposed to walk. Mom and Dad don't care . . ."

The room became quiet as a tomb. The four of them looked everywhere except at one another.

"Well . . ." The grandmother finally broke the silence. "I know your mom and dad let you do all sorts of things. They're so into their work. . . ." She shook her head like a puppy who's just gotten out of a pond and motioned toward the kitchen. "Let's have a feast to celebrate your deeds, like Pancho said." She handed cookies all around. "I'm sure you three want to be off on your next quest."

Dom almost choked on the cookie she'd just slipped into her mouth. There was the friend thing again. She planned to rescue many people in distress. But really, as much as she wanted more friends, she couldn't bring each one of them along after the rescue. She didn't have enough money in her piggy bank for two people. How could she feed three? Or more? And her steed? Steph lived in a nice house with flowers and a porch. She didn't even live in an apartment house. She had a grandmother who made delicious cookies.

And besides, what if they took Steph along and Ponsi Bublassi didn't keep his word?

It would mean Pancho was right.

It would mean Dom hadn't saved Steph.

It would mean Dom wasn't a very good knight.

Ernie Bublassi could laugh at her forever.

She wouldn't have any grand adventures to share with Abuela.

"Maybe we can come by and tell you of our adventures," Dom said. "Play with you after our quest."

"I still limp, but I can walk fast. Give me a chance—you'll see." Steph's eyes darted from the knight to the squire, but she didn't whine.

"You can take my wagon in case she gets tired," the grandmother said.

Pancho stepped in front of Dom. "Steph didn't slow us down on the way here. If she gets tired, Roco could pull her in the wagon!"

"No, he can't. He's a dog, not a horse."

"I'll pull the wagon, then."

"I'll send a bag of cookies, with you," the grandmother offered. "For your quest."

"Cookies, yes," Pancho said, tugging at Dom. "Cookies would be wonderful."

Dom raised her hand. She intended to slap the kitchen counter where she was seated to make her point. It was just that a knight couldn't pick up every person she rescued. She was about to tell them about how the bully had promised to leave Steph alone.

Instead, on the way down, three of her fingers brushed an upturned lid. The lid swirled. And rang. And showed itself for what it truly was.

"The Golden Helmet of Membrillo!" Dom yelled.

"The Golden Helmet of Mem*what*?" Steph asked.

"Membrillo, Membrillo. It's most valuable. Don Quijote was looking for it. Every knight is looking for it. We are so lucky we found it!"

"It's the lid to a pot," Pancho said. "And it's 'Mambrino,' not Membrillo. Membrillo is in the middle of guava paste!"

Dom stopped. Pancho was right. Membrillo was in Abuela's favorite dessert. She had it every night after dinner. No wonder Dom had confused the name! She had seen the shiny brownish gel every day when she'd handed it to Abuela.

Still. She had found the precious helmet.

"Mambrino!" she said, trying out the lid on her head. "The name doesn't matter. I know Don Quijote backward and forward. The crescent moon marks this helmet as the famous one."

"The crescent moon marks a place for a spoon when the lid is on the pot," Steph said.

"You don't know what you're talking about! Neither of you." Dom directed herself to the grandmother. "Since Steph will be joining us on our adventures," she said, "would you be willing to let us have this priceless—priceless—"

"Lid," Pancho finished.

"Of course." Steph's grandmother grinned. "I'd be most delighted if you would take it with you. Along with Steph."

Dom turned to Steph. "What—what job do you think you'd like to have?"

"I know. I know." Pancho jumped up and down. "How about master of the cookies?"

"Just so," Dom said, and they prepared to leave.

The Golden Helmet of Mambrino! It was a great reason to bring Steph along. Pancho would be happy, and maybe Steph would turn out to be a friend. And that also meant that Dom didn't have to take on every other person she rescued.

Unfortunately, she was so happy about the helmet of Mambrino that she almost forgot the bully.

But the bully didn't forget her. Ponsi Bublassi

leaned against a tree across the street from Steph's house, twirling a twig in his hand.

"You gave your word!" Dom yelled. "Scram!"

The bully flicked the twig at her. "I'm so scared of you, error-knight!"

For a second, all four of them stood frozen.

Even Roco's tail stopped wagging.

Then Steph stepped toward the bully. "I'm not afraid of you," she yelled. "My new friends will protect me."

Steph turned and walked away.

Pancho's mouth dropped.

Dom blinked.

Roco barked.

"Yeah! She's not afraid of you." Pancho punched his fist in the air. He followed Steph.

"Yeah! She's not afraid of you!" Dom repeated even louder.

But then she stopped.

What had she done? If Steph had stood up to the bully, that meant Steph had taken care of herself. Dom couldn't take credit for saving her.

She still wasn't a fearsome knight.

She still needed an adventure to prove she was a worthy knight.

Something that would shut Ernie Bublassi up forever.

Where could she find a spectacular adventure?

"Giant," she said as she caught up to Steph and Pancho. "We have to fight a giant."

"A giant," Pancho Sanchez said.

"A giant," Steph echoed.

Pancho stopped and faced the knight. "And where—where do you think you can find a giant?"

"At the corner of Washington and Twenty-Seventh. Not far."

"I've never heard of a giant around here."

"You'll see."

A Delicious Detour

Dom and Roco led the parade. Steph followed. Pancho brought up the rear with the wagon carrying cookies, the saddlebag full of water and supplies, and the Golden Helmet of Mambrino.

They heard the crying before they figured out where it was coming from. A loud wail.

"Someone in distress!" Dom turned her head to tune in to where the sound was coming from.

"I thought we were on our way to fight a giant," Pancho said.

"Can't leave someone in distress! It wouldn't be right."

"Maybe the giant could wait," Steph said.

They followed the sound for almost a block and found a little boy sitting by a fire hydrant. Another boy stood next to him, licking a Popsicle.

Dom ran toward the crying boy. "Dom Capote to the rescue!"

Roco charged along and screeched to a stop. Right at an orange Popsicle quickly melting into

a pothole. Roco downed it with one loud, satisfied slurp. He left only a stick, smeared in orange.

"Whaaaaa!" Crying-Boy bawled harder.

"Roco!" Dom said, as if by yelling at him he'd give the Popsicle back. It didn't happen. She turned to the boy. "What seems to be the trouble, young knave?"

Crying-Boy stopped crying and scrunched his forehead.

"She means why are you crying," Pancho translated, which made the boy start howling again.

"He dropped his Popsicle and now he doesn't have one," said the other boy, who looked a lot like Crying-Boy. He caught the drips from his own Popsicle with his tongue before they hit his hand.

"Can you buy him another one?" Dom thought that could be a solution.

The brother shook his head. "Mom only gave us money for two."

"Mmm." Dom thought some more. "How about if you share yours?"

"And lick the same Popsicle?"

Dom shrugged. "Might help him stop crying."

"Ugh!" said the brother.

"Double ugh!" said Pancho.

"Triple ugh!" said Steph.

Roco licked his lips. Loudly.

All three of them stared at Crying-Boy. He needed something to let him forget the lost Popsicle.

"Master of the cookies." Dom's voice boomed over the wailing.

Steph straightened up.

"Cookies!"

The master of the cookies handed treats all around. She gave Crying-Boy five extra cookies.

The wailing stilled to a whimper, then stopped. No-Longer-Crying-Boy got busy chewing.

"Success!" Steph held out her hand for a high five.

Dom was happy No-Longer-Crying-Boy was no longer crying. But was it enough of a deed?

She was about to tell the others she knew this was not a feat worthy of a fearsome knight when she stiffened. Ernie and Ponsi Bublassi had sneaked up to them.

"I heard there was a knight loose in the neighborhood," Ernie said. "Guess that's what girl-knights do, huh? Hand out cookies!"

"Buckethead's the bravest!" Ponsi bowed low.

Dom straightened up. "Knights take care of every need, big and small!" She looked at her squire, her steed, and her master of the cookies. "Onward!"

12
A Giant

Dom Capote and Roco rushed toward Washington Avenue and took a right. With confidence.

Her squire and her master of the cookies followed, looking back at the two bullies. With dread.

Ernie and Ponsi Bublassi followed at a distance, laughing. With anticipation.

"There!" Dom shouted as they neared Twenty-Seventh.

"The giant?" asked Steph.

"Whoa! Where?" Pancho asked. "I don't see a giant."

"There. In the park. At the corner. Next to the restaurant." Dom pointed. "Look at the size of its arms. Look at them whirling in the wind!"

Roco barked at the four whirling blades, which almost swept the ground.

"That's no giant. That's a windmill."

"That's exactly what Sancho Panza told Don Quijote," Dom said. "But Don Quijote fought the giants and won!"

"Maybe Don Quijote fought giants," Pancho said. "But this is a windmill. It's the Holland House Restaurant!"

"It's not real," Steph said. "Look at the size of the restaurant. The giant's not even two stories tall. The giant in 'Jack and the Beanstalk' was *ten* stories tall."

Dom glared at her squire and her master of the cookies. Her forehead scrunched. Her mouth set.

Pancho got very close to her.

"Ernie's watching. He won't believe that's a giant,"

he whispered. "See the mother on the bench? She's changing her baby. Her other kid is playing. A mother wouldn't let her kids be around a giant, right? This is just a restaurant in the corner of a park."

Pancho was right, but Dom didn't have a choice.

There hadn't been any good knightly type adventures in Mundytown.

At least she was doing exactly what Don Quijote had done. Fighting a windmill.

She had to try.

Tomorrow was Monday. It was her only chance. "It'll have to do." Dom took a deep breath, pointed her lance, and broke away. "Prepare to meet your Maker!" Screaming, she charged. And jumped over the little fence surrounding the giant.

Roco followed his knight, barking.

Pancho and Steph launched themselves toward the windmill. They planned to help.

Unfortunately, instead of clutching Dom from certain doom, Steph and Pancho tripped over the fence, smacked into each other, and fell in a heap.

At the giant's feet. They pushed Dom's lance into the giant's arm swooping by.

"Leggo, you fiend!" Dom joggled her lance so violently, the turkey baster came loose. The lance snapped. Dom flew back onto Pancho and Steph.

That's when she heard the woman scream.

And saw the little boy.

Running by the windmill.

Straight toward the street.

"No, no, no, no!" Dom sprang between the blades, leaped over the fence, tackled the toddler like she'd seen Rafi do at football games, and in one very swift motion, gave him to his scared, and relieved, mother.

"Thank you so much!" the mom said.

Dom grinned. "Of course! What are knights for?"

She looked back just in time to see her squire and her master of the cookies beginning to move. And stand. And stumble. Straight for the giant's arms, instead of away from them. Their steed circled them, barking.

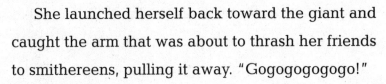

She launched herself back toward the giant and caught the arm that was about to thrash her friends to smithereens, pulling it away. "Gogogogogogo!"

They did.

Pancho grabbed Roco as he and Steph stepped away from the giant and outside the little fence.

Dom let out her breath. She let go. The giant's arm gave a jolt. With a terrible crack, it snapped as it glided by.

Tug! The giant snagged the hood on Dom's cape.

Rip! The cape tore.

Whoop! Her foot slipped on the escaped turkey baster.

Ouch! Her ankle screamed.

Ooof! Her bottom hit the sidewalk.

From the ground, Dom watched her cape flap at the end of the giant's arm.

So much for the Knight of the Cape.

The door to the restaurant opened. "What's going on here?" a woman demanded.

Dom followed the woman's eyes. The windmill's blades still whirled, but two of them were bent, like puppets' arms. She was the knight. She had to take responsibility. But what should she say? That she was pretending to fight a giant so that Ernie Bublassi would believe girls could be knights? That she had broken the windmill to prove a point even though they all knew it was a windmill and not a giant?

She didn't have to figure out what to say.

"She saved my Bobby!" The little boy's mother was almost crying. "I was on that bench right there. I was changing the baby. I didn't realize he'd run away till he was ready to hit the street. There's no way I could have stopped him." The woman pointed at Dom. "She did."

"Yes, she did!" Pancho said loudly, aiming his voice toward Ernie and Ponsi Bublassi. "Without a doubt, Dom Capote, the Knight of the Cape, saved another person in distress."

"And she did it without any help!" Steph gave Ernie and Ponsi Bublassi very knowing looks.

Dom's whole body was shaking and her eyes were scratchy. Everyone around her was cheering, except, of course, for Ernie and Ponsi Bublassi. They were across the street. Mouths gaping. Watching.

Dom stood next to the woman and looked up. "Are you the owner?"

The woman nodded. "I'm Ms. Belle." She was tall. One of her feet was tapping as if she were ready to take off.

"I stopped the arms so my friends wouldn't be hurt." Dom blinked hard. She guessed the movement she could see out of the corner of her eye was the two bullies getting closer. She couldn't let Ernie Bublassi see what was filling her eyes. "I'll be glad to come sweep your sidewalk every morning and afternoon until I pay for whatever I broke."

"No problem, honey!" Ms. Belle's hand dismissed Dom's offer. "Those blades are meant to snap off."

Dom's eyes widened. Snap off. She hadn't broken them.

"The good thing is you saved that little guy. He would have been squished on that street for sure!"

Dom's shoulders relaxed. Her fists loosened up. A long sigh slipped from her lips. The Knight of the Cape had saved the toddler. She could hold her head up. She had done it. Dom Capote, girl-knight, had really saved a person in distress. And she hadn't broken the windmill!

"Come on," Ms. Belle said. "Let's see if everybody's okay and I'll fix the blades."

"Wait!" The squeal escaped out of Dom's mouth. Then she lowered her voice. Looking at the two bullies standing at the corner where Bobby had almost gone into the street, she told Ms. Belle about Ernie Bublassi. And wanting to prove girls can be knights.

"So you're a knight?"

"Like Don Quijote."

Ms. Belle gave Dom a high five. "You go, girl!"

Dom smiled. "Could you take our picture? With the little boy? You know . . . so we have proof?"

"Of course we'll take a picture. You deserve a medal. You rescued this little boy. And everyone needs to know about it. I'll send it to the newspaper. Girl-knights rule!"

The boys were getting close to Steph. Dom motioned for Ms. Belle to get close to her. "Can you say that again, a little louder?"

The owner of the Holland House Restaurant did, looking straight at Ernie and Ponsi. And then she added, "You guys lose anything around here?"

No answer.

"Maybe you'd best quit gawking and go home!"

"Away!" Steph added. "You don't belong by this worthy knight!"

Pancho punched his fist up into the air. "And never get near us again!"

Ms. Belle's mouth broke into a grin. "We'll take the pic in a sec! But first, let me make sure nobody's hurt."

She walked over to Pancho and Steph. "You both okay?"

Pancho rubbed the big goose egg on his forehead. "I'm fine. Just a little bump."

Steph nursed a matching bump. "Little? You have the hardest head in the universe!"

Dom didn't say anything about the throb in her own ankle. Or laugh at Steph. She still couldn't believe she'd rescued a real person.

"I'll bring you some ice," Ms. Belle said. "Just hang on."

She came out a few minutes later, holding two Baggies of ice, a remote control, and a phone. She pushed a button on the controller to stop the blades and stuffed it into her pocket. She handed out the ice. Then she started posing people.

"Come on, come on, everybody in front of the door, here. By the sign. I want a picture for the *Mundytown Weekly.*" The woman swept her hand in front of her, pointing to an imaginary headline: *"Local Students Save Runaway Toddler!"*

She arranged Dom in the middle, lance in hand. Pancho, holding Roco, she posed on Dom's right. Steph on her left. She placed Bobby right in front of Dom.

She took one picture and checked it out. "Perfect!" Then she took four or five more. And a couple with Dom's phone. "They'll be on their way to the

Weekly tonight," she promised. "And now I think it's time for some lemonade."

Dom touched her on the arm. "One more picture? With the windmill?"

"Whoa, girl! I can't have pictures of my restaurant with a broken windmill out in the universe! I don't have time to fix this right now. I have a house full of people wanting to be fed. I'll take care of it later."

Dom wanted to beg. She wanted proof she'd been just like Don Quijote. Exactly like Don Quijote.

But the owner of the Holland House Restaurant had said the word "broken."

The word pinballed inside her head.

What if the blades really had broken? What if her friends had gotten really hurt? What if Bobby hadn't made her a hero?

"Mmmm, you look a little green." Ms. Belle got down, level with Dom, her dreadlocks brushing Dom's forehead. "You know why I can't do it, right?"

Thoughts crowded Dom's head. The woman was the farthest thing from her mind. "Yeah . . . yeah . . . I get it. . . ."

"Good. I'll bring the lemonade."

Dom hesitated. "I . . . We don't have any money."

The owner threw her head back, laughing. "It's my treat, brave knight!"

Dom still hesitated.

Pancho stepped in front of the woman. "That would be delicious!"

"Us knights are supposed to celebrate, aren't we?" Steph said.

"Absolutely," Bobby's mother said. "Bring out some cookies, if you have them. They'll be my treat. It's only right."

"How about I bring them out here?" Ms. Belle pointed to a picnic table. "That way you can stay with your dog."

"Our steed," Dom barely whispered.

"Your steed—why didn't I think of that?" Ms. Belle opened the restaurant's door. "I'll bring them out in a sec."

13
A Perfect Knight's Story

Dom was still in a funk when they were ready to leave the Holland House Restaurant.

Pancho bowed to the restaurant's owner. "We thank you for your bounty, most kind castellan," he said to her. Then he turned to Bobby's mother. "And you, too, kind mistress."

Dom tried to shake the cobwebs from her head. She needed to thank the owner of the Holland

House too. "Yes, thanks so much. Especially . . . you know . . ." Her fingers took an air picture.

Ms. Belle broke into a huge grin. "Us girls gotta stick together."

Dom gave her a half wave, and she, Pancho, Steph, and Roco set off toward home.

Dom leaned on her broken lance as a cane for her twisted ankle. Each step reminded her of how much worse the whole thing could have been. And how close she'd been to having Ernie Bublassi laugh at her for the rest of her life. And having no exciting adventure book to share with Abuela. In the beginning, the book for Abuela was a way to get Rafi to help her, but now it really meant a lot. Who would want to hear about a granddaughter whose only exciting deed had been to rescue bunnies?

"What?" Pancho punched her in the shoulder. "What's with the grumps? You did it. You're the most amazing knight in the universe."

Dom shook her head. "I'm not a knight, and I didn't fight a giant. I could have broken that windmill. Really broken it. Like a million dollars' worth of broken. And what if you were hurt? Or Steph? Or Roco? That little boy came out of nowhere. What if I hadn't been able to stop him? I would have had no adventures for Abuela. And Ernie Bublassi would have laughed at me for the rest of my life."

The three were silent for about five steps.

"It was all my fault," Dom muttered. "If I hadn't tried to fight a giant, none of this would have happened."

Steph spoke up first. "It's the other way around. If you hadn't tried to fight the giant, Bobby might have gotten hurt. You wouldn't have been there to save him."

"And you stopped the blades from smashing into us," Pancho said.

Dom didn't even look at him when she answered. "That wasn't a big deal. They were meant to break."

"But they were hard. They tore your cape off. Maybe we would have gotten all tangled up in there or pushed against the windmill. We might have broken something if you hadn't stopped the blades."

"You saved us," Steph said.

"It was a stupendous battle," Pancho said.

"You were brave."

"Totally valiant, O wondrous knight." Pancho bowed low.

Dom smiled. She was happy they were trying to make her feel better, but she knew for sure Bobby was the one who had saved her.

★ ★ ★

The three stopped at Dom's house.

"We had a wonderful adventure," Pancho told Rafi after he introduced himself and Steph.

"We did not," Dom said. "This little boy was running out onto the street. And I stopped him. I looked like a hero, but we're lucky I didn't get us killed or have to pay millions of dollars to fix the Holland House windmill."

Pancho and Steph told the story. The more they talked, the more exciting the adventure seemed, even to Dom.

"Hold your heads high!" Rafi said. "You did amazing deeds. Deeds worthy of the best knights of the realm. And you rescued a real person. You kept him from harm. Let's have the pics. I'm going to write all about it."

Dom shook her head. "We did nothing."

"Oh, no, no, no," Pancho told Rafi. "We haven't told you the best part yet. Thanks to Dom Capote, we own Ernie Bublassi and his brother, Ponsi. Gone. History. They'll never torture us again. Maybe they won't even torture anyone else again."

"Yeah, right!" Dom said. "The only way we'll be rid of the Bublassi brothers is if they move to Pascagoula or somewhere."

Pancho wouldn't let it drop. "But you said . . ."

"That was Don Quijote. I'm for real now. And I know Ernie Bublassi won't ever leave us alone."

"We're rid of them for a while anyway," said Pancho. "You proved girls can be knights. The picture will be in the *Mundytown Weekly*, right? We'll be famous. Whatever Ernie says, we can point to that picture. Everybody in Mundytown will see it."

Rafi leaned forward. "Wait. The picture will be in the *Mundytown Weekly*?"

Dom shrugged. "The owner of the restaurant said she was sending it to them."

Rafi gave Pancho a high five. "Oooh, maybe they'll publish my story. If they get a picture from her and a story from me, you will really own Ernie Bublassi. He might try to mess with you again, but you can put your nose up in the air and walk away. You showed them! In the weekly paper!"

"Yeah . . ." Dom heard what her brother was saying. It was making its way into her brain.

Steph stepped up. "They'll never bother me again," she said. "I have friends now, don't I?"

"I watched you save that little Bobby," Pancho said. "You were like a lightning bolt! If you hadn't tackled him, he would have ended up in the street, squished by a car. I promise."

Dom straightened up.

"Well, there you go." Rafi jumped up on his bed and spread his arms wide. "You know what? You wanted to prove you were a knight and you did! I get it. You were exactly like Don Quijote! Most of the time he messed everything up just like you. Even if you hadn't saved the little boy, you did what you said you would! You were a knight. Just like Don Quijote."

Dom smiled. "All I know is if Bobby hadn't run away, Ernie Bublassi would be laughing his head off. I'd never be able to set my foot in school tomorrow."

"But he did, didn't he!" Rafi said. "And you saved him. And everything else you did was like Don Quijote."

"Even the bunnies?"

"Well . . ."

Dom was shaking her head.

"I have an idea," Rafi said. "Let's call Abuela. She'll tell you whether you're a good knight or not."

They put Abuela on speakerphone and pushed the story over the airwaves.

"Oh my," Abuela said. And "exciting." And "amazing." And then the best thing was: "You were just like Don Quijote!"

"Exactly!" Rafi said. "That's what I told her."

Abuela didn't remember what she had for lunch, but she could still remember things that she knew a long time ago. "Rafi's right. Don Quijote didn't always succeed in what he started out to do," she said. "But he always tried to do the right thing. The thing a good knight would do. He tried to help. And that's what you did. And then you actually rescued someone! You're even better than Don Quijote."

Dom grinned.

"And I can't wait to have the book so I can read it to all the other grandmas in my building! They'll be so jealous that my granddaughter's a knight!"

After Rafi hung up, he pulled out his laptop. "Let me hear it again. So I can finish the book. Everyone must know about your deeds, especially the *Mundytown Weekly*."

So they told him again. Every little detail. He typed furiously. The way Rafi wrote it, even Crying-Boy and his brother sounded exciting.

As soon as he finished, Rafi printed each of them a book of their knightly adventures, each illustrated with eleven pictures. He put one in an envelope for Abuela and printed another one for their parents.

"Mami and Papi will just love this!" Dom said.

The last thing Rafi did was send an article to the *Mundytown Weekly*.

"Now they'll have a story to go with the picture. That should be proof enough for Ernie Bublassi that a girl can be a knight!"

"And just in case, Dom and I can pass our books around in class tomorrow," Pancho said.

That night, before going to sleep, Dom read Rafi's book. He was right. She had been like Don Quijote.

She had messed everything up. But things didn't turn out as bad as they could have. And she had done it. She had set out to do something and she'd done it. She had been a brave knight. Along the way, she had saved little Bobby. And that felt good. Tomorrow she could show everyone in her class her book. But the icing on the cake was that her picture would be in the *Mundytown Weekly* that Thursday. As the hero. She had shown Ernie Bublassi!

Most important, Abuela would also have a copy of the book soon. She could read it to her new friends. It would give Dom and Abuela adventures to talk about.

She was still looking forward to rereading more of the books Abuela liked. But something had changed. Pancho turned out to be a brave and excellent squire. Steph turned out to not be a damsel at all. Reading about adventures was fun, but it was better to have real adventures with real friends.

She put *Dom Capote's Knightly Adventures* by Rafi Melendez in her bookcase, next to her other adventure books—the ones Abuela had brought from Cuba. As she did, she noticed a book sticking out, as if waiting for her. *Treasure Island!* Girls could be pirates, too, right? She reached in a drawer for a bandanna. She tied it around her head and texted Abuela.

Pirates next. Stay tuned.

Author's Note

The Knight of the Cape is similar to *Don Quijote*, (*Don Quixote* in English) a book written by Miguel de Cervantes in the early 1600s. Don Quijote is a man who, like Dom, likes nothing better than reading. People tell him he shouldn't read. Especially people in the church. But he doesn't pay attention. He imagines he is a medieval knight and sets out to look for adventure.

Don Quijote finds a squire named Sancho Panza, who keeps him real like Pancho Sanchez keeps Dom real. Like Dom, when Don Quijote rescued someone, he thought the tormentor would never come back. He tackled bullies like Ponsi Bublassi and thought he'd won. Both Don Quijote and Dom fought giants that were actually windmills.

Rafi said that Don Quijote, like Dom, messed everything up most of the time. And that's exactly what happened. At the end of their knightly adventures, both Dom and Don Quijote face the truth about themselves. But unlike Don Quijote, who dies at the end of the book after having set his life right, Dom goes on. With two new friends, she sets out for other adventures based on other books.

Acknowledgments

Mil gracias de mi corazón. To my Reston writer's group: Teddi, Judy, and Kim, for helping me birth Dom and her band; and to Cathey, Della, and Michelle, way back when, for giving me the confidence to pursue my dream of writing. To my Arlington writer's groups: Thank you for taking me on and sharing your love, suggestions, and patience. To Jacquie, for always reading everything I send her way, and to all my Guild friends for welcoming, supporting, and encouraging me. To SCBWI Mid-Atlantic: Thank you for providing fertile soil in which to grow.

To Natalie Lakosil, my agent: Thank you for believing in me and for your ability to turn a sow's ear into a silk purse, as well as other superpowers. You are always on my shoulder.

To Aly Heller, editor extraordinaire, for in-person and virtual hugs. For believing, like me, that kids of all skin tones, ethnicities, nationalities, religions, and genders need to see themselves in the pages of children's books as no different from their peers. Thanks for your gentle touch.

To Mari Lobo and Fátima Anaya, who see Dominguita exactly like I picture her.

To my kids and grands: Your love and pride keep me afloat. MK, thanks for insisting Dom Capote should be a girl.

To Lou, forever my love, cheerleader, and champion: You're the one who makes it all possible.

Turn the page for a sneak peek at Dominguita's next adventure!

Definitely DOMINGUITA
✕ Captain Dom's Treasure ✕

by Terry Catasús Jennings
illustrated by Fátima Anaya

1

What Dom Found in the Book

Dom was at the Mundytown library when it opened. She wore a bandanna around her head, squishing her pigtails. And a leather eye patch with a shiny gold *P* for "pirate" covered her eye. Her brother, Rafi, had given her the patch before she left home. Along with a compass.

"Nice look, Dominguita!" Mrs. Booker, the librarian, looked up over reading glasses. "What can I do for you?"

"Captain Dom," she corrected. "You know Dominguita means 'little Sunday' in Spanish, right? No one will respect a pirate named after a day of the week!"

"Sorry for that, Captain Dom. I can see how that could be a problem." Mrs. Booker straightened some papers on her desk. Then she nodded. "You continuing your pirate studies?"

Dom didn't quite know what to say. She still loved the books Mrs. Booker had given her. The ones about Anne Bonny and Mary Read—the best pirates ever. And she didn't want to hurt the librarian's feelings. "I'm not done with studying. Honest. But I think we're ready to actually do something, you know? Like look for treasure."

"Treasure?"

"Me and my mates. Pancho Sanchez and this new girl who's visiting her grandmother. Her name's Steph. We're going on a pirate adventure."

"I see."

"I need two copies of *Treasure Island*. One for

each of them. You can't be a pirate without reading *Treasure Island.*"

"I can't agree with you more." Mrs. Booker touched the mouse in her hand to wake up her computer. "You already checked the shelves?"

Dom nodded. "Couldn't find any. My brother, Rafi, agreed to make us a treasure map, so that we can actually look for something. But we want to really act like pirates."

After a few clicks, the librarian shook her head. "We do own two. . . . Looks like someone checked them both out a couple of days ago."

"Hmm," Dom said. "How about another library? Anything close?"

"Wait, wait. We have our Special Books Collection in the basement. I think we have one there." She reached for a notebook swollen with yellow, curling pages. "The librarian before me couldn't get rid of some books. I loved her for it."

After turning a few pages, Mrs. Booker gave a little happy cry. "Yep. Looks like we're in luck."

If there was anything Dom liked better than a book, it was an old book. She kept twelve adventure books her grandmother had read as a little girl in the bookcase next to her bed. They were ready to fall apart, but she loved every one of them. Even though her abuela had moved to Florida, the books made Dom feel connected to her in some way. Dom read them all the time. There was no way she'd miss a chance to go down to the basement to see other old books.

She followed Mrs. Booker down the twisty steps without being invited. The smell in the stacks made her as happy as the smell of sweet buñuelos.

And it made her sneeze.

Which startled Mrs. Booker.

And made her look back.

Caught!

"Sorry, sorry, sorry," Dom said. "I know I shouldn't have come. . . ."

"Are you kidding?" Mrs. Booker said. "You're welcome here! I love this place too!"

The librarian stopped at a table that stretched from side to side at the end of the room. The label above it said SPECIAL BOOKS COLLECTION. Books were piled four deep in neat columns. The first book Dom saw was *Little Women.*

"Mmmm." Mrs. Booker's fingers ran over the columns. "*K, M, R.* It should be here." She stopped at the fourth column over, bottom row, and lifted books until she found the one she was looking for. She blew the dust off the cover and handed it to Dom. "See, I told you it was beautiful—all yours."

This was a good time to start using pirate talk, Dom thought.

"It'll be pure gold to me, I promise."

✕ ✕ ✕

With a wave, Dom left the librarian. Pancho and Steph were waiting for her at Yuca, Yuca, the restaurant that belonged to Pancho's uncle. El Señor Prieto had agreed to feed them during their recent knightly adventures if Dom swept his sidewalk.

She should run. Her mates were waiting, ready to set out on the treasure hunt.

But something about the old book called to her.

She wanted to touch it. Smell its oldness. Take it all in.

By herself.

She stopped at a table by the door and traced the gold letters on the red cover with her fingers. They were barely raised, rounded. She opened it. Carefully. As if it were holy. It was printed in 1947. A couple of years before her abuela was born.

It was not like any other book she'd read. It was crackly, yellow. Some of the type was fancy. Very fancy. With full-color pictures of fighting pirates and black-and-white sketches scattered in the chapters.

Dom thumbed through the loose, worn pages. And there, between pages 168 and 169, she found a flyer. Folded. Pink.

An advertisement for Kowalski's Grocery!

Dom smiled. Mr. Kowalski had helped in their knightly adventure too. He'd made her a knight!

Next to Kowalski's ad was one for Beauty Is You! on Grant Street. That beauty shop was Smart Clips now. That's where Dom's mami got her hair cut. The bottom half of the flyer said the carnival would be in Mundytown from June 20 to June 23. What year? It didn't say. Not on that side. She flipped it over.

And stopped breathing.

On the other side was a map.

X marked a spot.

2
What Dom Did at Yuca, Yuca

Dom barreled into Yuca, Yuca. Her breathing exploded in short, loud bursts. "I. Found. A. M-m-map. Ifoundamap. Ifoundamap."

"Whoa! Whoa! What about 'Shiver my timbers' and 'Ahoy, mates'?" Pancho was tall and hefty. He wore a twisted bandanna to hold the mass of black hair on his head away from his forehead. A plastic sword hung from his belt.

"You mean Rafi already gave you the map?"

Steph scrunched her forehead. Her freckles danced. She was not dressed like a pirate.

"No. No! Well, yes. We have a map." Dom drew her crew into a huddle. "But not from Rafi. I have something better. Just now. At the library. I found a treasure map. A real treasure map!"

"But why don't we wait and use Rafi's map?" Steph said.

"This treasure map is *real*. I promise!" Dom whispered, holding up the book. "I found it between pages 168 and 169."

Dom didn't wait for her mates to answer. "It's like the map in *Treasure Island*. It has notes and two *Xs* and the numbers ten and thirty-seven."

Now Pancho and Steph nodded. Maybe they were getting it.

"I can't wait to pretend to find the treasure with it," Steph said.

"THIS IS NOT PRETEND!" Dom yelled. "THIS IS A REAL TREASURE MAP!"

Everyone in the restaurant looked up. Her mates. El Señor Prieto. The cooks and waiters. Even a blond girl who was having flan at ten o'clock in the morning.

Dom straightened up. "It's a real *pretend* treasure map, Steph. Rafi made it for us. You're right." Her voice was the most normal she could manage. And loud. So everyone could hear her. "And WE NEED TO WEIGH ANCHOR AND SEARCH FOR IT. RIGHT NOW." She pulled her two friends out of their chairs and through the door of the restaurant. She ran. She didn't stop until she was three blocks away. She knew she should have waited for Steph, but it was as if she were being pushed by a hurricane. Finally, she stopped in an alley between apartment buildings, where she plopped down on the steps by a back door of a building.

✗ ✗ ✗

"What was that all about?" Pancho asked, panting, after he and Steph caught up to her.

"I can't believe I blabbed! I told everybody about the map."

"But isn't it a pretend treasure map?" Steph dropped next to Dom.

"It's not!" Dom cried. "It's real. Real. Real. I know it is. And now everybody knows we have a *real* treasure map."

Pancho waved her off. "Don't worry. Nobody pays attention to us. They don't care."

"But I talked so loud!"

Pancho shrugged. "Last week we were knights. This week we're pirates. My uncle knows we're playing. Everyone knows we're playing."

Dom sighed. "You think?"

"Sure. Nobody takes us seriously."

"Oh." Dom wasn't sure which was worse, giving away the secret or that no one took them seriously.

Steph patted her on the back. "Come on, Cap'n," she said. "Show us the map!"

Dom pulled it out. She held the precious paper by the corners. Her fingers shook as she smoothed it out on her lap. Even with the noises of the street, their breathing was all she could hear.

Steph whistled. "Could be for real."

"It's real," Pancho agreed.

Dom grinned. "I told you!"

She traced the shape on the paper with her index finger. A rectangle. Sort of. One of the two long sides was missing a half circle. As if someone had taken out a chunk with a cookie cutter. There was a small x. There was also a larger X, in blue. It was north of the small x.

Which was only north if you agreed that the random, half-finished arrow on the right of the paper pointed north.

Which may not be a good thing to agree to.

Because it looked more like a chicken's foot.

And there was absolutely nothing else that showed north.

Whoever drew the map scattered four lines with circles on top—like lollipops—inside the rectangle. The number thirty-seven was an addition. In different ink.

But then, at the bottom of the page, scraggly, like the X, a note: *The sun will show when it's highest in the sky. Dial, diagonal, park.*

In neat handwriting: *Ten feet from X to x.*

All three stared at the paper for more than a minute. Dom broke the silence. "Wow, huh? It's good enough to yell *huzzah!*"

Pancho nodded. "Shiver my timbers, it's a puzzle."

Steph shook her head. "But it doesn't say where this is. It could be on another planet."

Steph was right. The buccaneers in *Treasure Island* knew where the treasure was. They had coordinates. They knew hills, and creeks, and coves. They could use a compass to find the place. But Dom still had a feeling this was a *real* map.

"So here's the deal," Dom said. "The flyer is about Mundytown. The book was in the Mundytown library. We look in Mundytown. My mami won't let me go anywhere else anyway."

Steph shook her head. "I just don't want to be going all over everywhere. That's why Rafi's map . . ."

Dom had to get Steph to agree, to get off this kick about Rafi's map. "I think gold dust of you," she told her friend. "I want you to be ship's doctor. That's the next most important post after captain."

Steph scrunched her face again. But it was a happier face.

"Whoa! I'm glad we're out of *that* clove hitch," Dom said.

"Knotty problem," Pancho translated before Steph even asked.

"Now we're getting somewhere, buccaneers!" Dom gave them each a high five. "Pancho, will you be first mate?"

Pancho saluted. "Aye, aye, Cap'n."

"So what do we need?"

"It talks about parks, right?" Pancho pointed to the map. "We need maps to figure out where parks are. And a compass."

"Gran gave me lots of maps so I won't get lost now that I'm living here."

"Rafi gave me a compass before I left this morning."

"How about swords and gullies?" Pancho asked.

"Gullies?" Steph asked.

"Knives," Pancho said. "Pirate knives. Pirates always have swords and gullies. Who knows? If we get hot on the trail of this treasure and someone finds out . . ." Pancho patted the plastic sword hanging from his belt.

"I'll see what I can find at Fuentes Salvage," Dom said. "But we might as well forget the gullies. I don't think he'll let us have any even if he has some."

"Shovels, pics, and stuff to dig treasure with," said Steph.

"Well, jump on the yardarm, Doc, that's a brilliant idea!"

"Lunch!" Pancho said. "I'll run back to Yuca, Yuca and get ham biscuits."

It was time to wrap things up, the captain thought. "Eight bells. Forenoon watch. Bring your stuff to the conference room at the library. I don't think we should meet at Yuca, Yuca for now."

"Aye, aye, Cap'n!" Pancho saluted, and turned to leave.

Steph followed him. "Wait, wait. What's eight bells, anyway?"

"It's ship's time," Pancho said. "Noon."

"I'm gonna have to read *Treasure Island* tonight."

"Watch the movie," Pancho said. "It'll be faster."